EL – MISTERIOSO

PART – 1

M. AJAY DEEPU

Copyright © M. Ajay Deepu
All Rights Reserved.

This book has been published with all efforts taken to make the material error-free after the consent of the author. However, the author and the publisher do not assume and hereby disclaim any liability to any party for any loss, damage, or disruption caused by errors or omissions, whether such errors or omissions result from negligence, accident, or any other cause.

While every effort has been made to avoid any mistake or omission, this publication is being sold on the condition and understanding that neither the author nor the publishers or printers would be liable in any manner to any person by reason of any mistake or omission in this publication or for any action taken or omitted to be taken or advice rendered or accepted on the basis of this work. For any defect in printing or binding the publishers will be liable only to replace the defective copy by another copy of this work then available.

Contents

Foreword   *v*

CHARACTER INTRODUCTION

   1. The Caller   3

   2. The Truth   11

Mr. Mad Story Universe   15

Foreword

"all the characters and events depicted are fictitious. Any resemblance to a person living or dead is purely coincidental".

CHARACTER INTRODUCTION

Joe : Biggest Bussiness man in India

Ginger : Servant of Joe

Harish : M.P of ruling party

Sarala : Wife of Harish

Rudra : C.I of Mumbai

Saraswati : Wife of Rudra

Bharat : Airport Head of Mumbai Airport

Sanjay : B.I.G transporters owner

Thomas : B.I.T distributors owner

Abhinay : P.A of Mrs. Shanti

Mrs. Shanti : C.M of Maharashtra

Abhishek : New C.I of Mumbai

Jay : A.C.P, of Mumbai

Manish Panday : D.G.P. of Mumbai

Mr. Mohan Rao : P.M. of India

CHAPTER ONE

THE CALLER

It was April 1ˢᵗ of the year 2022. It was around 2:30 AM at night. Mr. Joe was sleeping peacefully

["**PHONE RINGS**"]

Joe wakes up and answers the call. Someone on the other side of phone call said ["**You are going to Die** "]

["**CALL CUTS**"]

Joe believed it was a prank call.

["**PHONE BEEPS**"]

Next day morning, Ginger was on his way to his master's house.When he reaches, he directly goes back side of the house and opens backdoor.[**IT WILL NOT BE LOCKED**]. He directl goes to kitchen and prepares breakfast for his master.After preparing breakfast, he calls his master loudly to come and finish his breakfast. He calls his master 3-4 times. But no response. He then walks upstairs to reach his master's bedroom. He finds that the door is not locked. He slightly pens the door, he was shocked by seeing blood n the floor. Then he fully opens the door, he was shocked by seeing his master lying dead on his bed with holding his head in his hands. He then rushes out and calls the police...............

["**AFTER 10 MINS**"]

Police had arrived to the crime scene. Ginger explains what was happened. Theyy were searching for clues. Then the found Joe's mobile phone. Te kept that mobile in the clue bag. After 1 hour news had spreaded to the media. All the civilians of Mumbai was shocked. Police had sent the body to the frenseic department fr post mortem.

Police department had handed over this case to Rudra. Rudra hired a technecian to unlock the mbile phone of Mr. Joe. He had sent the phne number of Joe to the cyber crime department t get call list. When the technecian unlocked the mobile, Rudra checks that phone for some clues. He opens the messaging app. He saw a message from an unknown number showing *"HAPPY DEATH DAY"* at sharp 2:30 AM. He was shocked. Rudra then asks cyber crime department to track that unknown number.

["AFTER 7 DAYS FROM DAY OF JOE'S MURDER"]

It was arund 2:30 AM at night. Mr. Harish was sleeping.

['PHONE RINGS"]

Mr. Harish did not bother to attempt the phone call.

["PHONE BEEPS"]

It was aroun 5:30 AM in the morning. Harish wife Mrs. Sarala returned from her maternals house. When she rings the door bell, no one responds. She uses the spare key of the house which is with her. When she opens the main door, she switches on all the lights, she left her trolley in the hall and walks upstairs to reach their bedrom When she opens the dor of their bedroom she screams by seeing her husband with holding his head in his hands.

Police department and media arrived to the crime scene. They all did their procedures and Mr. Rudra had found Mr. Harish's mobile phone. After finding it, he asks Sarala to unlock his husbands mobile phone. After unlocking, he immediate goes to the messaging app. He checks the messages. He finds again the same message *["HAPPY DEATH DAY"]* at sharp 2:30 AM at night.

["RUDRA PHONE BEEPS"]

Rudra opens his phone and checks his phne. He got a message from the cyber crime department. He then opens the photo of post mortem report f Mr. Joe. When he reads the details , he was shocked, because the murder happened at sharp 2:30 AM.

He was in confusion. How a person can send a message and kills the person at same time?.

Police department was on confusion. D.G.P. Manish Panday has kept intense pressure on Rudra. The next day morning , forensiec department had sent the post mortem report to Rudra's station. Rudra opens and reads the report, he was shocke again as the again mentioned that Harish died at exact 2:30 AM. Rudra was full tensed.

["7 DAYS LATER"]

It was aroun 10:30 PM at night. Mr. Rudra after finished his works, he was on his way to his house. When he reache his house, his wife Saraswati tells him to fresh up fast to celebrate their 14th wedding anniversary. He freshed up and came down to celebrate .

["AFTER 1 HOUR"]

Rudra went to his work room to investigate deeper in these cases. He was thinking and trying to find some clues.

["AFTER 2 and half HOURS"]

Due to work tension , he felt asleep. It was around 2:30 AM.

["PHONE RINGS"]

Due to tiredness , he didn't bother about that phone call.

["PHONE BEEPS"]

It was 5:30 AM. Saraswati ha woke up and started to clean his house. After cleaning the house, She freshed up. After freshed up she saw the clock, it was 6:30 AM. She walks upstairs to wake her husband. When she tries to open the door , it was not opening. She pushes harder and harder, after some struggle, she manages to open it. When she opened the door , she shouts "Aaaaaaaaaaaaaagh".

Rudra was lying dead by holding his head in his hands........

Police team reached to the crime scene. D.G.P. was shocked. Now Mumbai people are not believing the police department that the could find the killer. The police department has no choice of choosing anone because everyone in the department were scared to take up the case. Then at that time Jay came forward to take up this case.

D.G.P has now took a deep breath in relief. Everyone in the department were shocked. Jay immediately asks D.G.P. to give him full powers an access to all files. D.G.P. agreed to his conditions. Jay immediately rushes to the station. His co-workers had welcomed him. Jay thanks them all and sits in his seat and asks his co-workers to bring the case files of Joe, Harish, Rudra.

He cross examines all the files, he got no clues. Then he asks his co-workers to bring the mobile phones of Joe, Harish and Rudra. He then looks into the mobiles deeply. He notes the common unknown number. He then asks them to send these details to cyber department, but one of them says that Cyber department failed to track or trace out the number. Jay then goes to the Joe's house. On his way , Jay tells to call Ginger for investigation

["AFTER REACHING"]

Jay started his hunt for clues. But he finds nothing

["GINGER ARRIVES"]

Jay asks Ginger to explain what was happened. Ginger explains everthing. Then Jay returns back to his office. While returning back, he saw CCTV camera at a shop opposite to Joe's house. He asks his co- workers to get the footage of the CCTV camera.

["AFTER GETTING FOOTAGE"]

Jay checks the footage , but he fins no one coming or going to Joe's house. It was around 7PM, with frustation Jay goes to his house.

["AFTER 2 DAYS"]

Ja continues his search for clues. But he gets nothing. It happens everyday and evertime when he tries to search for the clues. Higher officials are stressing and applying intense stress and pressure on Jay.

["AFTER 5 DAYS"]

It is a nice breezy day. It was around 8:30 PM. Bharat completes his duty and returned to his house.

It was arond 2:30 AM. Bharat phone rings. Due to tireness he didn't answer it.

["PHONE BEEPS"]

Next day morning Bharat didn't attended to his work. Like this it happened for three days. A foul smell is coming from Bharat house. Neighbours compalined about this to the police department.

Police arrived t the house , when they opens the bedroom door, they were shocked to see Bharat lying dead with holding his head in his hands. His body was rotten. Police had informed about this issue to Jay. He immediately arrives to the crime scene. He was shocked. Police team had did their procedures.

["AFTER 3 DAYS"]

Ja deeply investigates the case files and backgrounds of these people. Thn he finds out that Harish property was more than a normal M.P.. He thinks that either Harish came from a wealthy family or he must did some illegal activities. Then he fins out the the history of Harish. There it goes , he actually had a 1 acre land but now he has 500+ acres. Mysterious!. Due to this mystery, he started to dig deep in his mobile to know how he got that much property. There goes another mystery. Jay found Joe's contact in Harish mobile. Then he took all the phones and searched, there goes another thing. He finds these three members have a link and these murders have a link..

He had called Ginger, Sarala for investigation

[INVESTIGATION BEGINS]

Jay : Ginger, tell me does Mr. Harish comes to your house?

Ginger : Yes Sir, he will come. when he comes, my master sends me out to not listen their conversation

Ginger : But one day Harish sir said *"when will they will deliver us?"* . My master said that they will deliver us soon.

Jay : Did your master said anything more?

Ginger : No sir.

Jay : OK, you may leave now.

Ginger leaves. Jay calls Ms. Sarala for investigation.

Jay : Mrs. Sarala, does CI Rudra comes to our house often.?

Sarala : Yes.

Sarala : But not only Rudra.

Jay : What do you mean

Sarala : Harish, Joe, Rudra, Bharat, Thomas, Abhinay and Sanjay are best friends

Jay : Who is this Sanjay, Abhinay and Thomas

Sarala : Sanjay is the owner of B.I.G International transporters, Thomas is the owner of B.I.T Distributors company and Abhinay was the P.A. of C.M. Shanti

Sarala : Sanjay will deliver the International goods to India and Thomas will recieve it and distributes to all over India.

Jay : OK, you may leave now.

Jay had told them to leave.

After with these serious investigations , he had fund out that these 6 members are best friends.

Now he knows who will be murdered next. But he is confused that who will dies next, Sanjay (or) Thomas . So he told his co workers to explain what will be happened next to Sanjay, Thomas, he also told them to arrange high security for them. Jay returns to his house.

It was around 2:30 AM. Sanja was in tension. He was walking around in his room.

["PHONE RINGS"]

Sanjay was scared to answer the call.

["PHONE BEEPS"]

It was around 6:30 AM. Jay was sleeping. His phone rings. He attempts the call clumsily. When he answers the call, he was shcked by listening the death news of Jay. He immediately freshes up and rushes to Sanjay's house. He was shocked by seeing Sanjay lying dead, holding his head in his hands. Jay was in confusion he don't know how the murderer passed these many polices and killed Sanjay.

He gets doubt whether Thomas is alive or not. He calls his officers who were guarding Thomas and asks them to see whether Thomas is alive or not.

The police team immediately goes in and checks whether he is alive or not. They were shocked by seeing Thomas lying dead. They immediately calls Jay and tells that Thomas is dead. Jay immediately arrives to the crime scene. He sends those to post mortem. He asks them to send the within two days. After sending those bodies, he to his station and asks them to bring the mobiles of those victims.

They brings those mobiles. Jay checks for clues, he finds one common contact named Abhinay. He immediately calls to that number.

Abhinay lifts the phone call.

Abhinay : Hello, P.A of Mrs. Shanti speaking here.

Jay : Oh, sorry wrong number.

Then Jay thinks that all these people have link with C.M or her P.A.

So Jay started to search deeply in their mobiles. Then he finds a private folder in Rudra's mobile. He tries to open it but it asks password. So he sends that phone to the cyber crime department to unlock that folder. They unlocks the folder. Jay see some photos in those folder. He opens it. He sees Rudra, Harish, Joe, Bharat, Sanjay, Thomas are making a deal with foreigners. Rudra also took a selfie with them. After seein those, he goes to the C.B.I. headquarters. He asks his friend to give the data of these foreigners. His friend took that phone and went to his cabin. After a long time his friend came out of the cabin.

Jay : Did you found anything?

Friend : Yes

Friend : These foreigners are the members of Evil's Society. They were very dangerous and be careful.

After hearing that he started to investigate about the Evil's Society. He spent so many on this. Jay was sleeping.

["PHONE RINGS"]

Jay answers the call clumsily. Then he wakes up with a sudden shock. He immediately freshes up and goes to the C.M's house. He was stunned by seeing the dead body of C.M. Jay was confused. He asks them that who saw C.M. lying dead.

Constable : Her servant .

Jay : Call her.

Servant : Sir ?

Jay : Are you the servant of Mrs. Shanti ?

Servant : Yes

Jay : Tell me what was happened.

Servant : It was around 8:30. I went to give bed coffee to our madam. I knocked the door but no response. I found it was opened. So i went in and was shocked by seeing our madam lying dead.

Jay : OK

Then the media arrives to the crime scene. They already started telecasting it live . Then after hearing the news all the party members, fans, followers etc, started riots on roads. They burnt so many busses , shops , trucks, and what not. After 47 years again mumbai was on high alert. All the people were scared and started to demand the gun licence for them. The Indian Electiion Committee appointed Jaya Vardhan as the new C.M of Mumbai. The new government was about to sanction the gun licence to everyone, then Jay came and adviced them to not sanction it, because the killer will kill them at any time if he want but our people will use the gun for other purposes like robberies, murders etc. He also asked them to give 7 days and within that he will find the criminal.

The new government accepted and gave him 7 days time..........

CHAPTER TWO

THE TRUTH

Jay came out and started investigation. He interrogated every member and didn't missed any detail. He was so stressed but he didn't give up. He didnt slept for three days. Finally he prepared a file named *"EL-MISTERIOSO"* . He took an appointment with all the chief justices of Supreme court. He went to meet them along with his file.

After appearing in front of them,

CJ-1 : Tell me why you wanted to meet us.

Jay : Respected Justice let me tell you that I've found the criminal.

CJ-2 : A criminal, who ?

Jay : The killer who killed those 6 members along with C.M. in mumbai.

CJ-3 : Who ?

Jay : Our Prime Minister, Mohan Roy.

CJ's : Are you mad?

Jay : No.

He submits the file to the Chief Justices.

Jay : Sir, when i checked the contacts of those 6 members I found a common contact-Abhinay. So I interrogated him unofficially and here what i've found. These people are the drug smugglers including C.M.. I too shocked by hearing this.

Joe had foreign contacts . One day he started to smuggle the drugs in India. His friend, Harish came to know about this and started o buy from him and sells those in his clubs secretly. Then they planned to sell these all over India. So they buyed Bharat, Thomas, Sanjay and Rudra . Their bussiness was going nicely but one Rudra's friend Abhinay came to know about this. So he too joined that alliance and C.M. came to know about this and arranged a meeting with them secretly.

They all feared that she will punish them, but instead of them she gave a masterplan and oredered them to follow this plan. The plan was, Joe will talk to the members of that bloody Evil's Society and takes a small sample. That sample will go to Harish, he will sell it in his clubs if it was ok then they will buy that in a large amount. That will be delivered by Sanjay from America to India and that package will come outside from airport by the help of Bharat and that package will be distributed by Thomas to all over India, Rudra will manages the Checkposts by buying some members.

CJ-1 : Ok then how Prime minister is linked with this.?

Jay : Coming to the point that our Prime minister has Roy group of Industries and internally he is the smuggler. While dealing with that society he came to know that these people are smuggling without his attention. So he called them and asked a 50% share from them. They didn't agreed for that . He blackmailed them and with no choice they agreed. That was fine, but our P.M didn't stopped with that, he recntly created an ***ANTI RED SANDAL SMUGGLING FORCE (ARSF)*** but that force is appointed with curropted officers and they started to smuggle it.

But one day our C.M. made a master plan. He was not giving the 505 share of P.M instead of that he is giving 25% and covering the truth. Finaly he came to know about that and started to scare them but one day they all fighted each other and P.M. was about to shoot the C.M but the other members stopped them and bet the Prime minister. Due to that he was so angry on them, he started to call them every night and blackmailed them.

Jay submitted the call record of the P.M

And he is the one who called them every night at 2:30 and killed them. But he forgot the fingerprints. He uses tha same weapon to kill them all but while placing their heads in their hands his fingerprints were there on those heads. So i gave an award given to me by prime minister to the forensiec lab. The fingerprints exactly matches to the award which I gave.

Jay submits the lab report.

Jay : That's all my lord.

All the CJ's discuused about this and sent a team to arrest the P.M and that ARSF squad members.

All the peole of India took a dep breath after finding the criminal. The Government had awarded Jay as the best Police officer.

[AFTER 1 MONTH]

Jay went to his parents house, they all congragulated him. He spent the day very happily. Jay was watching the T.V then he saw the news that the vehicle in which the PM and that members were arrested that was blasted, Jay smiles and turns off the T.V . It was around 2:30 AM. Jay was sleeping peacefully in his room.

["PHONE RINGS"]

Jay didn't respond to that call......

Next day morning his mother walks upstairs to wake him up. When she opens the door, she screams Jay...........

[AFTER 10 MIN]

Abhishek along with his team ariived to the crime scene. They were shocked by seeing Jay without head . Then they finds a notice stuck on his body, when they take and reads it they were stunned by reading that , it states-

"It is not an End , It's just a Begining"

EL -- MISTERIOSO CONTINUES................

Mr. Mad Story Universe